1 2 3 4 5 6 7 8 9 10
❖
First Edition

HAROLD and the PURPLE CRAYON™

The Birthday Present

Adaptation by Valerie Garfield
Illustrations by Kevin Murawski

 HarperFestival®
A Division of HarperCollins*Publishers*

Harold couldn't sleep.

His mother's birthday

was the next day.

Harold didn't know what to give her.

He wanted to find the perfect

birthday present.

Harold didn't think he could find it

in his bedroom,

so he picked up his purple crayon

and set off on an adventure.

Harold decided to go for a walk.

He drew a path

and started on his way.

Harold drew a tree.

It was such a nice tree

that he drew one more,

and one more,

and one more.

Soon there was a forest.

Harold walked under the trees.

They were so tall

they stretched up to the sky.

Harold didn't know which way to go.

Harold climbed to the top of a tree

and looked in every direction.

But he couldn't find his way out.

Harold knew what to do.

He drew a bird

and flew to the edge of the forest

on the bird's back.

Harold came to a stream.

On the other side,

he saw a big field of flowers.

Harold drew a bridge

and crossed over to the other side.

Now the sun was high.

It was very hot, and the flowers

were sleepy and droopy.

16

The flowers needed water.

Harold reached as high as he could

and drew a big rain cloud in the sky.

The cloud blocked out the sun.

Drip! Drip! Drip!

Rain came down from the cloud.

Harold drew an even bigger cloud.

Drip, drop! Drip, drop!

The rain poured down on Harold's head.

Harold drew an umbrella

as quickly as he could.

The flowers weren't thirsty anymore,

but they still looked droopy.

Flowers need water and . . .

Sun!

Harold drew a gust of wind

to blow the clouds away.

The sun sent bright rays
of sunshine down to the flowers.
One by one they lifted their heads
to the warm light.

Harold looked at the pretty flowers.

His mother loved flowers.

Flowers would be
the perfect birthday present!

24

Now Harold had another problem.
He couldn't take the whole field
home with him.

Harold had an idea.

He thought of the perfect gift.

But it was at home.

How could he get back?

Then Harold remembered

that he could always see the moon

from his bedroom window.

Harold drew his bedroom window
around the moon.

Back in his bedroom, Harold realized
that the perfect gift for his mother
had been right at his fingertips
the whole time!

Harold would give his mother a flower.

He knew she would love it.

She could keep this flower forever,

and it wouldn't need water or sunlight.

When Harold finished the flower,

he left the picture where his

mother would see it.

Then he climbed into bed.

Then Harold dropped off to sleep.

And Harold's purple crayon

dropped to the floor.